The wise eagle
Hate
Yggdrasil
Freya and her cats
Hugin and
Munin
Idun
Balder
Frigg
Mime
Loki
Odin on Sleipner
Mime's Well
The Well of Wisdom

VIKINGS

Text and illustrations by

Siv Grøstad

based on an idea
and in collaboration with

Helge Nordskar

Translated by Pat Shaw

J.W. CAPPELENS FORLAG A·S

Printed in Denmark
ISBN 82-02-16655-1

CONTENTS

THE MYTH OF THE CREATION

Once at the dawn of time, when everything was chaos, Ymir the first jotun appeared. Tremendous, primeval forces met. Ice and fire surged together and

formed a barren, rime-covered landscape. Audhumla, "the rich hornless cow", gave the first jotun milk. Because this was a jotun, the first giant in the beginning and he appeared before the gods. Ymir was both male and female, and while he slumbered his primeval sleep, jotuns and monsters began to emerge from his body.

Suddenly, the first god was standing in the midst of the flock of jotuns. He was radiantly fair, and big and strong. He had been licked out of a block of salt. Time passed. Gods and jotuns multiplied and lived side by side in Ymir's rime-covered world. Among the gods were three brothers. They were tired of Ymir and the jotun chaos. Their names were Odin, Vili and Ve. They killed Ymir. The giant's blood became a mighty flood which swept everything along in its path. Only a few Jotuns survived. They escaped in a meal-bin, and sailed into Jotunheim. From Ymir's enormous carcass, the gods created the world. The blood became rivers and seas. Knuckles and bones became rocks and mountains. The flesh became soil and the maggots in the flesh became dwarves. From the skull they made the vault of heaven, and four dwarves were placed in each corner of the world to hold it up. Their names were North, South, East and West. Then they threw Ymir's brains up in the sky, where they became heavy, threatening clouds. They created the Sun and the Moon and the stars from the sparks in Muspellheim, the realm of Surt, the fire jotun. The Sun and the Moon were given separate paths in order to keep Night, the Jotun daughter, apart from Day, the son of the gods.

When everything had been arranged, the brothers wished to create some creatures who could live in the world. Creatures who resembled themselves. Creatures they could care about and rule over. It was then that they discovered two logs lying down by the shore. They were of ash and elm, and resembled two lifeless figures. Odin bent down and breathed life into them. Vili gave them understanding and movement. Ve gave them shape and speech, hearing and sight. The gods had created the first man and the first woman. They were called Ask and Embla.

SPRING ON THE FARM

The seed is ready for sowing. Winter is over and everyone is happy to be able to work out of doors. The farmer's son has taken the horse in order to ride around and gather people for the spring work. Many were needed now, because it is hard work to plough and work the land.

The mistress of the farm is eager to get the sowing done. All the men talk about is the next Viking expedition. But mother takes charge, and tells them what to do, in order to finish the work before the men depart. She is already thinking about the coming winter. Will there be enough food for the household and the animals? It is she who carries the keys to the store-house, and must see to it that there will be enough food for everyone.

THE MYTH OF HEIMDALL

Heimdall, the god, wandered over Bivrost, the rainbow bridge, to Midgard. He called himself Rig when he came among people. The path led to a hovel where Ai and Edda were sitting by the fire. These were Great-grandmother and Great-grandfather. Ai and Edda received the stranger warmly, as fair and handsome and radiant as he was. They were very old, with gnarled hands and crooked backs. They made room for him at their humble table, and shared their food with him. Rig stayed in the hovel for three days and three nights, before he again took up his pilgrim's staff.

Edda had a son by Rig. He had huge hands and a coarse face, a bent back and protruding heels. He was called Thrall. He grew up and

learned everything about hard and menial tasks. Later, Thrall met Tir, and from these two are descended all the serfs.

Rig continued to wander in nooks and crannies, along the road in Midgard. At last he came to a hill on which there stood a manor. He went inside and found Ave and Amma busily working by the hearth. They were Grandmother and Grandfather. Rig was given a proper reception. He slept with them for three nights. Then he set out again on his travels.

Amma gave birth to a son after the nights with Rig. He was ruddy-cheeked and had alert eyes. He grew and thrived, learned to make carts and drive a plough, build houses and

tame oxen. In time he married Snor. From them are derived the peasant stock.

Rig continued to wander along the road in Midgard. It swung up onto a promontory with a view in every direction. Here stood a great hall. Rig went inside and greeted them. He was received by Mother and Father. Cloths of patterned linen were placed on the long table. Roast fowl, veal and thin wheaten cakes were borne forth on silver platters. Wine was poured from jugs. Rig stayed for three days and three nights.

Jarl was the name of the boy which Mother had by Rig. His eye was as keen as an eaglet's. He learned to swing a shield and make arrows, hurl spears, ride, fence and swim. He rode into battle, won great lands and was generous with gifts. Jarl wedded Erna, and the two had many sons. The youngest of these was named Konungr. Konungr learned all kinds of sports and military games. He learned the language of the birds and had the strength of eight men. From Rig himself he learned the Runes. Konungr became a king.

A SACRIFICE TO NJORD

The day has arrived. A light breeze skims along the fjord. At last he will be allowed to take part in a Viking expedition. The boy reins in the horse. How skittish it is today. It is a good thing that his father can calm it down. There is the smell of the sea, of dried fish and tar. The ship bobs up and down on the waves, and the ropes and planks creak. The thralls carry barrels and boxes on board. There is a great deal that has to go on the long ship. Perhaps they will be on the great sea for many weeks. And sixteen men need a lot of food and drink. Under the floor boards they stow furs from the winter hunting.

Njord, the god of the sea, stands on the burial mound, gazing to the west. The Vikings gather around him to make a sacrifice. They have chosen a large bull for the god. Perhaps he will give them good fortune in their trading with the furs. But first they must cross the sea, and then they need protection against the evil spirits.

NJORD AND SKADE

Skade came barging, fully armed into Asgard in order to avenge her father, the jotun Tjatse, who had been slain by the gods. The gods stared at her, spellbound. They had never seen such a fearless jotun woman before. Then they suggested that, as compensation for Tjatse's death, Skade should be allowed to choose a husband from among the gods.

But before she made her choice, she could only look at their feet. Skade stood and contemplated the bare feet of the gods for a long time. "I must choose the prettiest," she thought to herself, and looked down at a pair of clean, little feet with well-formed toes. "These are most certainly Balder's feet, and Balder is the fairest of them all." She cautiously poked at a toe with the tip of an arrow. "I'll take him," she said

It wasn't Balder, but Njord from Noatun. Skade was not pleased. The gods had to make her laugh before she would agree to this marriage. The gods thought this was quite impossible, because Skade was as stubborn as a winter storm. But then Loki, the great mischief-maker, found a way. He tied one end of a rope around the beard of a billygoat, and tied the other end around his genitals. Both tugged and both howled. In the end, Loki tumbled into Skade's lap. Then she roared with laughter, and this is how it came about that Skade and Njord were wed.

Skade belonged to the mountains and Njord was the god of the sea. They could not live together, neither in Noatun nor in Trymheim. So they moved apart. Njord remained in Noatun, where he could hear the shrieking of the seagulls, Skade rushed to her mountain home. But after the marriage with Njord, Skade has been called the "Ski Goddess"

FROM A VOYAGE

The storm tears at the mast and sails. The rain lashes against the face. The hands are numb with cold and without strength, where the Vikings stand clinging to the ropes. The dragon's head shoots up towards the sky, on the foaming crest of a wave. Here it nods briefly to the gods, before it plunges down in the depths, towards the bottom of the sea. This is Ran's kingdom. She is a jotun woman, cunning and greedy, and as hideous as a monster. Is Ran casting her nets now? They had carved runes on the bow as protection against evil powers. Nonetheless, they can sink, and then everyone is lost unless he has gold in his pockets. The chieftain has a lump of gold in the right place.

He, at least, will be well received by Ran, if they should sink. There is supposed to be a great hall on the bottom of the sea, which abounds in dazzling gold and glitter, so that no light is needed there. Ran has nine beautiful daughters. In a storm they appear as frothing crests on the waves. The sight of them over in the churning water makes him shudder.

He vows to sacrifice his best horse to Njord, if only he survives this voyage.

THOR FISHES THE MIDGARD SERPENT

Once, Thor assumed the guise of a young boy, and journeyed to Jotunheim in order to visit Hymir. Hymir got up at the crack of dawn and was going fishing. Thor was ready to accompany him, but Hymir felt he was too little to go so far out to sea. He thought Thor would freeze to death. Thor was furious. It was just before he killed Hymir with his hammer. He wouldn't be the first to turn the boat back to land, he sputtered. Then Thor went into the forest and wrenched off the head of Hyme's biggest ox. This would be suitable bait, he thought.

Once they were on board the boat, Thor started rowing so fast that the sea foamed about the bow. It wasn't long before they had reached the fishing ground where Hymir usually caught halibut. But Thor wanted to go farther out, and lay into the oars. "There's a danger of meeting the Midgard Serpent here," whimpered Hymir, so the icicles jangled in his beard. But Thor would not listen, and kept on rowing. At last he pulled in the oars, and threw out the line with the ox's head on it. It sank into the depths. Hymir quaked. Suddenly, the line jerked so hard that both of Thor's hands slammed against the gunwale. At the same moment, he summoned his divine power, and braced his feet through the boat until they were standing on the the bottom of the sea. Thor struggled and pulled until the sea was churning. He had caught the Midgard Serpent itself on the hook. When he had hauled the terrible head over the gunwale, he seized his hammer. For a second, the world's worst enemies glared at each other. Now, Thor thought he had won the battle. He only had to smash the hammer into the skull of the beast. But Hymir became so frightened that he took his fishing knife and cut the line. Thor stood and watched the Midgard Serpent disappear into the depths.

AN ATTACK ON A MONASTERY

War cries mingle with the sound of sword against shield. An army of wild warriors storms ashore. They want the gold and all the precious objects which the monks have hidden. Some of them have managed to escape, and are running into the forest. They know they don't have to run very far, because the Vikings usually remain close to their ships. The monks have little to match the weapons of the Vikings. They are brutally slain. Young girls and boys near the monastery are taken prisoner. With hands tied behind their backs, they are flung into the ships. They are made into thralls and lose their freedom. Not long afterwards, the ships head for the mouth of the fjord.

LIFE IN VALHALLA

The Einheriar were seated around the table in Valhalla with Odin. These had been great warriors, chieftains, jarls and kings when they lived on earth. They had fallen in battle, and the Valkyries, Odin's warrior maidens, had brought them to live with Odin in Valhalla. There they fight each other, die and come back to life every evening. The same thing happens every single day. This is the way they are preparing for Ragnarok, the end of the world. Then they will be Odin's good warriors in the battle against the jotuns.

Every evening there was a feast in Valhalla with the best food and drink imaginable. The cook was named

Andrimne, and every day he slaughtered the boar Særimne, in order that the Einheriars would have enough to eat. The next morning the boar was just as alive again. From the udders of the goat Heidrun, the mead flowed in great streams. She stood on the roof of the hall, and her udders were always full. But Odin himself did not eat. He sat deep in thought, and drank only wine.

New Einheriars came to Valhalla, because in Midgard, in the world of men, war and strife prevailed. The Valkyries rode over the battlefields, and always picked out the bravest warriors for Odin.

KAUPANG

The Jarl has not come to deal in thralls. He has enough back home on the farm. To be sure, they work hard enough, but they are a burden to feed. Suddenly, he pulls up his horse and stares. There stands the most beautiful girl he has ever seen. The jarl must remind himself why he is here. "Thrall woman for sale!" the trader shouts in a broken dialect. No! He wasn't going to have a new thrall. The jarl had come a long way to barter his winter furs for beautiful glass and the sweetest wine.

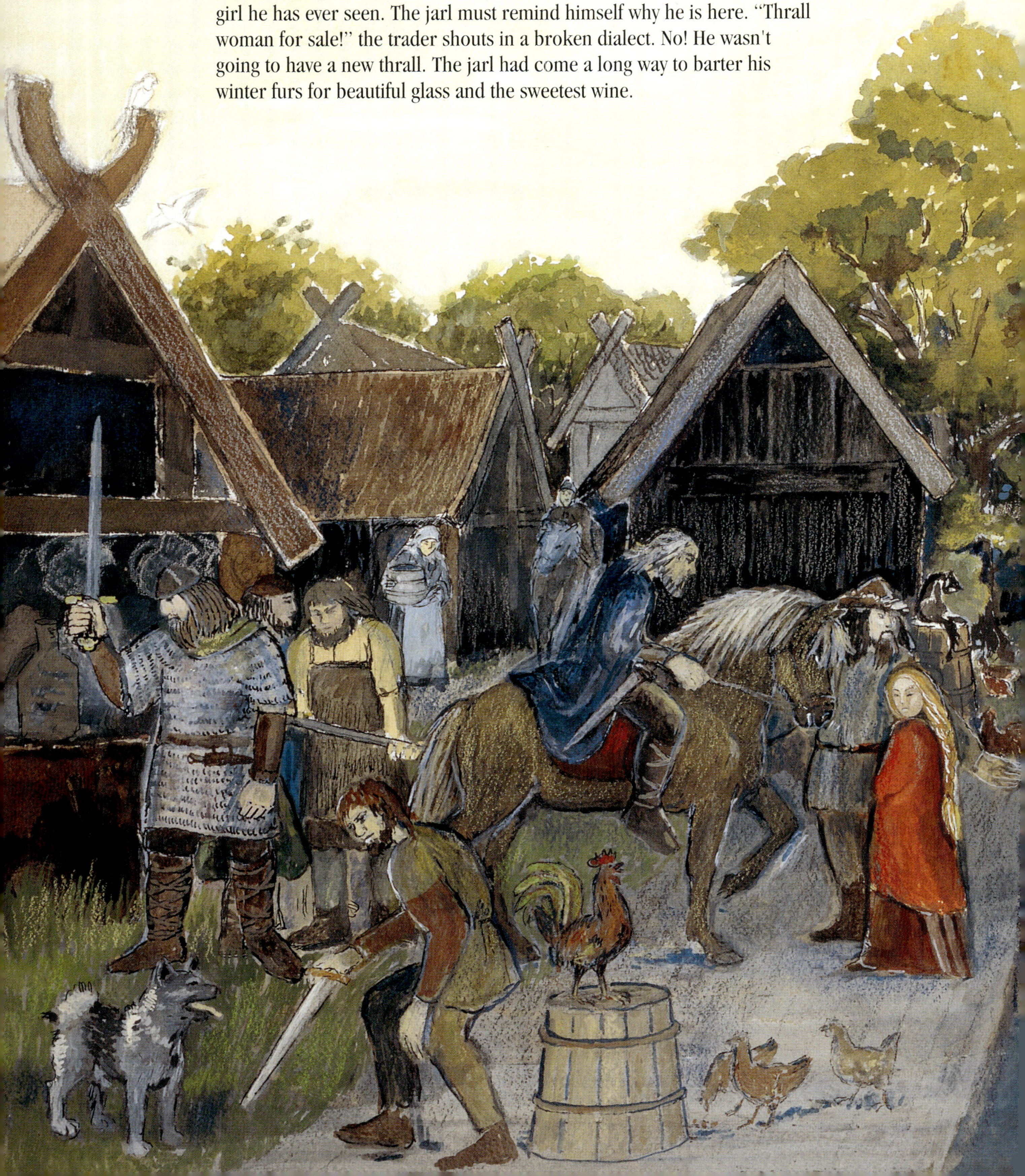

For a moment, he is at a loss what to do. It is as if he has drunk the strongest mead. "Take her home as a concubine?" he thinks. No and again no! His wife is of noble birth.

Before he knows it, he is in the midst of bargaining. The thrall woman is not cheap. Half of the pile of costly furs goes in payment.

THE MYTH OF FREYA

Once, when Freya was wandering in Alfheim, she discovered a grotto deep in the forest. When she went to have a closer look, she discovered four dwarves who were making the most beautiful necklace she had ever seen. It shone and glowed in flaming gold. When she asked to hold it, she saw that it was a masterpiece, a treasure the like of which she would never find again. Freya knew at once that she had to have this necklace. She wanted to

bargain with the little men, and offered both silver and gold and great quantities of precious objects. But the dwarves were both cranky and contrary. They had plenty of gold. At last Freya became angry and hissed, "What do you want, then?" "Well," said one of the dwarves whose name was Berling. "If the goddess of love can give us a night of love each, then the necklace will glow around Freya's neck. Freya agreed to this. For four nights she remained in the grotto of the dwarves. After the final night, the four skilled craftsmen accompanied Freya out at the crack of dawn and fastened the precious Brisingamen around her neck. In the glow of the necklace, the morning sky blushed and the morning star shone like a diamond. And wherever the goddess went, it was reflected in the colours of the rainbow, in the clouds and in the gold of the sunset over the sea.

THE THING

The law speaker raised his staff. A mighty chieftain has asked for the hand of a beautiful farmer's daughter in marriage. Patiently, she stands waiting with her flaxen hair flowing about her blue robe. "Will I wear the keys to the chieftain's manor in my belt?"she thinks. "He is not exactly handsome, nor is he young. But he is rich and powerful." The tension mounts among the people at the Thing, or assembly. Her father gravely approaches the circle, with heavy steps. His men lay their swords in the grass outside the sacred ring around the Thing plain. Peace shall prevail inside the ring, no matter how much they lose their tempers. "It's a good thing that not everything has to be decided with blood," she thinks. For several generations there have been disputes between their families. Power and honour have always been at stake. It is often the women who egg them on. The men fight and many lose their lives. If her father agrees to this marriage, there will be a reconciliation between the families. She knows how difficult this is for him. She puts her faith in the Lawspeaker. He is wise.

She closes her eyes for a moment and prays to Syn, the goddess who sees to it that no one tells a lie. At the same moment, she knows that her wish will be granted.

THRYM STEALS MJØLNER

Thor had to dress up in wedding clothes. He was boiling with rage. Freya fastened the Brisingamen necklace around his neck, and now he was going to pretend to be the goddess of love. Loki could hardly wait to get started. "The bridegroom is waiting," he shrieked with laughter. This did not put Thor in a better mood. First, Thrym had stolen the precious hammer from him while he slept. And now he had to go to Jotunheim disguised as a bride. There could

be no greater shame. "No one gets the hammer before I get Freya as my bride," Thrym had sworn. But Freya would never be Thrym's bride on this side of Ragnarok!

The goats tugged and pulled at the shafts of the chariot. Now they had to get started in order to put an end to all this nonsense. Thrym stood and stared in the direction of Asgard. Wasn't his bride coming soon? The thunder rumbled and the lightning flashed. Now he glimpsed a chariot with both bride and bridesmaid. Then he shouted to the jotuns: "Scatter straw on the benches, jotuns. Now they are bringing Freya to me as my bride." And not long afterwards the wedding feast was ready.

The bride stepped into the jotun's hall, and behind her minced the bridesmaid, Loki. Jotuns are easy to deceive, and it didn't take long before Thor was sitting with his hammer in his lap. He seized the handle and swung it about him so the jotun blood flowed. He avenged himself both properly and well, in Thor's fashion.

A BURIAL

The Volve is dead. She is to be buried in her ship. An endless procession of people, old and young, poor and rich, wander along the bog where the ship is to be sunk. It will not be easy to bid farewell to someone who has meant so much to them all. For years, she has been the guardian of the temple of the gods, and has taken care of peace and fertility. She has travelled around in the districts healing the sick, helping women giving birth and conjuring away sorcery. She listened to everyone and always gave advice. Life will be empty without her.

A young girl walks close beside the cart. She has been apprenticed to the Volve, and some day she too will be a volve. This is a difficult task. But she knows that as long as the goddess is with her, she will manage it. She looks at the face of the dead woman. "How beautiful the Volve is," she thinks. "No wonder she was allied with Freya."

Two spirited horses drag the heavy wagon over the tussocks in the bog. They will also accompany her in the ship to the kingdom of the dead. She will also take along food and her most important possessions. "Perhaps the kingdom of the dead is at the bottom of the bog?" the girl thinks. "Since the ship is to be sunk right here." A burial mound will be built over the ship. This will be the new sacrificial site, and in this way they will be able to preserve the power of the Volve.

A cold autumn wind tears at the fir trees and carries the strains of the flute over the landscape.

THE SKALDIC MEAD

Once, the dwarves made a mead that was so precious that everyone who drank of it gained wisdom and a gift for poetry. There were many who wanted this drink, and there were many who fought for it. But no one could have it. Because now it was hidden deep inside the mountain of Suttung, the jotun. There sat his daughter, Gunnlod, and watched over it day and night.

Odin thought about Suttung's precious mead, which was standing unused inside the mountain of the jotuns. No one could benefit from it there. He wanted to bring the drink to Asgard so that it could be beneficial to men and gods. So he set out on a dangerous journey in order to get hold of the drink.

Deep inside the mountain Gunnlod sat guarding Son, Bodn and Odrerir, the three huge vats of mead owned by her father. One day she had a visitor, even though she knew that no one could find the way in to her. Odin had accomplished the impossible. She was so happy. In her confusion, she offered him the precious mead. Odin stayed with her for three nights, and drank everything that was in the three vats. Then he transformed himself into an eagle, and flew away from empty mead vats and a sorrowful jotun maiden.

Now, the Suttung mead was in Asgard. Odin gives the mead to the good skalds. For this reason, Odin was also the god of the skaldic poets.

THE MID-WINTER SACRIFICE

It is the winter solstice and freezing cold. Tonight they will have the mid-winter sacrifice. Relations and friends have gathered at the farm. They make their way up to the burial mound. They look to the gods and their ancestors to strengthen the ties, honour them and ask for help to get through the long winter.

They hunch themselves up against the wind. The ash spreads its black branches towards a hazy moon. Mighty, ancient and gnarled it stands, and bends over them as if to protect them from evil. The howling of wolves can be heard in the distance. Has the Fenris Wolf escaped? The wolf that will slay Odin one day?

Then the ceremony begins. Drums and rattles keep time, and the chants and the ram's horns resound. Pigs and horses are sacrificed. Splendid sacrifices are repaid in kind. Perhaps they will get what they pray for: A good year and peace.

BALDER'S DEATH

Grief and lamentation. Balder was really dead. And now Ringhorne, his great ship, was being prepared for his final journey to Hel, in the kingdom of the dead. Great numbers of gods, crowds of jotuns, indeed, all kinds of beings gathered for the funeral. But when the gods wanted to push the ship onto the water, so the voyage could begin, they were unable to budge it from the spot. Even Thor, the strongest of them all, was tiny under the mighty ship. Then they sent word to Jotunheim for a giantess named Hyrrokkin. She came riding on a wolf, with rattlesnakes as reins. Four berserkers had to hold her steed when she dismounted.

A single shove from Hyrrokkin was enough to send the ship flying over the water so the sparks flew and the whole earth quaked. Thor was green with envy, and was ready to cleave her skull. But the gods asked that she be spared, so he had to calm down.

Then Balder's body was carried on board and they placed the body of Nanna, his wife, beside him. The funeral pyre was lighted, and Thor consecrated the fire with his hammer.

A BIRTH

If it is a girl, she will be exposed. The farmer is master of his farm, and there are already too many mouths to feed as it is. Winter came early this year, and the autumn harvest was poor. No, he does not want yet another daughter. The birth was long and difficult. He thought his wife was going to die. It was then that the women sent for the Volve, the prophetess. She was allied with Freya and other goddesses. She knows runes, and about magic herbs.

It is a girl, after a long, difficult birth. The new-born baby has already been placed on the earthen floor. In this way she acquires vitality. He can hear it by her voice.

Suddenly, he feels how difficult it is to expose this girl to the wolves. He must ask his skald for advice. "Now, Freya has saved both mother and daughter. Let the Fates decide," the skald says. "The Volve believes that your new daughter will bring you good fortune. Go and adopt the child, and give it a name so the women can prepare the Lying in porridge."

RAGNAROK

The wolves devoured the Sun and Moon. The world was plunged into eternal darkness. Gullenkambe (Golden Comb) the rooster crowed from Yggdrasil and roused Odin's warriors to battle. Heimdall blew on Gjallarhorn, Hel's blackish red rooster began to crow, and Fjalar answered from Jotunheim. The old earth shook to its very foundations. Ragnarok was at hand. From the darkness of Hel, the ship Naglfar, made of the nails of dead men, glided out.

Then the heavens split asunder. With fire raging before and behind them, Surt and the sons of Muspell came charging over Bivrost the rainbow bridge. Rym the jotun came from the east with all the frost giants, and the ravenous Fenris Wolf at the head. The Midgard Serpent had writhed ashore, and rushed along with fire and venom spouting from its jaws. Thor fought the Midgard Serpent, Heimdall fought Loki. Odin was devoured by the Fenris Wolf. And Surt hurled fire wherever he went. The earth burned and was destroyed. The ancient prophecy had been fulfilled.

But after Ragnarok, a new world will emerge from the sea. Balder shall return from Helheim, and Liv and Livtrasse will come from Hoddmimesholt. They came from the old world and survived Surt's fire. From them, the new human race will be born.

Sun
Arvar and Alsvinn
Skoll
Thor and his billygoats
Tanngnjost and Tanngrisne
Jotunheim
Utgard
Bivrost
Njord
Asgard
Heimdall
Midgard
Ratatosk
Verdande
Urd
Skuld
Kvergelmir
The Well of Death
Urd's well
The Well of Fate